JAMES ROBERTSON

SOUND SHADOW

B&W PUBLISHING
EDINBURGH 1995

First published 1995
by B&W Publishing
Edinburgh
Copyright © 1995 James Robertson
ISBN 1 873631 49 9

The publisher acknowledges subsidy
from the Scottish Arts Council towards
the publication of this volume.

British Library Cataloguing in Publication Data:
A catalogue record for this book is available
from the British Library.

Cover design by Winfortune & Associates

Some of these poems have previously appeared
in the following publications:

Akros, Cencrastus, Chapman
Lallans, New Writing Scotland
Radical Scotland, Verse
The New Makars

Printed by Biddles Ltd.

CONTENTS

This book was completed when I was Writer-in-Residence at Brownsbank Cottage near Biggar. My sincere thanks are due to Biggar Museum Trust and to the sponsors of the Brownsbank Fellowship: the Scottish Arts Council, Strathclyde Regional Council, Clydesdale District Council and Waterstones's Booksellers.

James Robertson
Brownsbank
January 1995

SOUND-SHADOW
—a region of silence
behind a barrier to sound.
(Chambers English Dictionary)

THE ROAD TO THE FERRY

Around this house, late summer,
With all the tourists gone,
And a car along the road
Perhaps twice in an evening,
The wild things come to life again.
It is the sounds of them mostly:
Rabbits in the whins, and a polecat;
Bats fluttering against the window;
And the looping call of wind
In the telephone wires.
Down on the shore the congregations gather—
Duck, geese, gulls—all bickering for space.
A white owl haunts the garden and his own
Flight paths, putting the fear of death
In anxious voles.
We watch him and admire.
All this nature is very reassuring,
As though secure behind the glass
Our comfort can never be disturbed.

But the sounds I want to talk about tonight
Are different all together.
I heard them first in my dreams,
Or at the edges of them;
Then one night I came to with a start, struggling
To place their strange familiarity.
Suddenly I knew!—They were there, outside,
Bulging in the narrow road like some mammoth herd,
Stamping, snorting, shuddering.
I was afraid.
(Of course this was before the coming of the bridge,
But long after the last drowned ferry—and people,
Mindful of that sad disaster, were still content

1

To take the long route round.)
Barely able to contain a shout of fear—
Or was it jubilation?—I sat upright in my bed
As they trampled past, those sounds.
Just beyond the house they left the road,
Snapping the fence as one snaps fingers,
Crossing the links to the firth.
Even at a distance of half a mile I could hear them,
First their shaggy fetlocks splashing in the warm shal-
lows,
Then their great shoulders rolling and heaving
As they swam that slender neck of the sea,
That ruffled collar, that vulnerable grace.

The noise diminished and I felt my limbs relax.
I could only imagine them after that,
Shaking themselves as they rose up
Out of the falling tide, lumbering on and on,
Beyond all thought,
Beyond the grief of our time,
The built waste and the wrecked,
And the broken heart.

I have never slept so badly since;
Nor dreamed so well.

THE DEAD-SHIP

The jolly ship's jig is over.
This was a hell on earth, on sea,
A barkful of bedlam that breathed from its holds
Demons roaring drunk and rank with malice.
Here even fever shrank from the ferocity
Of its intended victims, a scab-eyed shifting crew
Whose rages flamed like running sores
From bow to stern, keeping the rats
Restless at night.
Ports denied them, not another sail in sight,
They got the worst of fear and clawed
Its scum into some shape of unbelief.
These men made scurvy walk the plank,
And when the last of the kail, rotten,
Dissolved its yellow ooze into the decks,
They slockened hunger with a poison dredged
From nameless kegs, put a mad match to their
Tinderous brains.
They sang *Let the sea take us, there is no truth*
But chance and the foul breath of an ill wind.

Their captain they caused to burn the charts,
And he, in turn, emptied his pistols under a table
Where a cheating man clenched cards
Between his knees.
Both were deemed too sane to be unsafe,
And were strung in the rigging like puppets
To creak and snap, and gather the salt hairst
Of the wind.
At length they were ghosts, or bleached angels,
While below them those few who were not drunk dead,
Nailed up by the limbs, or gibbering rudderless wrecks,
Fell to a final brawl, as pirates do,

And bled stale blood under a burnt sky
Into a single pile bloated and heaving with brutality.
Now the ship lists on, funereal, dumb with horror,
The black flag flapless, dance all done,
Silence shattered and a squeeze-box spilled out
Groanless on the deck.
Blindly she slides in the slow thick sea,
Bound for rocks she has no need of striking.

THE COLONEL SPEAKS, 1968

The Colonel jabs a finger
Under the collar of his square-bashed shirt,
And pulls it round to the relief of his throat.
Like Mafeking, or Lucknow, or just going on parade.
The stiff discomfort reassures his quivering lip.

Cake crumbles at the corner
Of the Colonel's mouth as he takes his tea,
His stubby grip bruising the fussy handle
Of the cup. He plops two lumps and some
Spillage in the saucer, grunts his thanks.

The occasional table for his side-plate
Looks unsafe. So does his wife.
The Colonel, crouched uncomfortably
On the edge of a flower-covered seat,
Looks set to spring on one or the other.

Already with his dry shorn neck
He's dislodged the antimacassar. Across the room
The women's aimless sofa-chat earns only his contempt.
They are like grazing, brainless antelope.
The Colonel sights imaginary shots at them.

He seizes then upon the small boy
Commandeered to pass his mother's scones—
"You, sir, what do you think?" His prey is barely ten
And overwhelmed by the noise, the tweeds,
The antiseptic smell. "No spunk," the Colonel thinks.

He drops a biscuit, laughs it off
With a snarl: always betrayed by his own unease,
His insecurity; the way he carried his rank
Into civilian life; his spluttering creed of discipline;
How he bullies his little wife.

Not that he has ever hit her—
There was no need. Not that she has ever
Asked for it. The dogs take all the beating.
Their marriage has no passion, no communication,
And a hippy daughter no one ever talks about.

Women! The Colonel looks again
At mummy's boy, resignedly allies with him:
They're the white men after all, clearly it's their burden
To show the women and the world its place
Here in this chintzy bourgeois drawing-room.

"Got an atlas, sergeant?"
(He's not averse to pulling rank on schoolboys.)
The boy, embarrassed, exits, shutting the door
On maternal hostess prattle and the thin whine
Of the Colonel's nervously behatted spouse.

He returns at length,
Clutching an ancient atlas which his prep school
Thinks still good enough—and despite the fees
His parents don't demur: they're paying after all
For privilege, not the finer points of education.

The boy is not so sure.
Reluctantly he proffers, expecting puce-faced outrage
At the maps, redundant and archaic.
But of course he's wrong, misunderstands
The righteous scowl. It's just what the Colonel needs.

"Look!" The Colonel orders,
Stabbing the world with his clumsy brazen fingers—
"And here!" at the red splashed over the centre pages.
"Hard to believe, isn't it?" Hard to believe.
The boy nods. "This, this, this . . . was all ours!"

PERFECT

For Anne

On a beach in Great Bernera

Beyond such a house at the end of a road,
Beyond a graveyard in so fine a place,
Beyond an island off a handful of islands
Squatting on the edge of the world,
I walked upon a pure white beach
Washed by a pure blue, ice-blue sea,
Thinking eternity.

Perfect.

A natural progression, laid out like a line of Chinese boxes
Marching into the sun-hung west.
And turning for a sign that you, too, understood,
I saw you point beyond again, your laugh
Like a flag in the wind,
At a single seal bobbing, nodding his head
To us, between the waves.

IN A BOOKSHOP

Three girls in a bookshop
Are fifteen. Their jewellery
Is manifest and cheap. Two of them
Bore rapidly, short laughs stretching
To giggles that say, "Let's leave."
The rows of books are too akin to Monday.
(They are fifteen, hung between two lives,
And each one hurts and each can be a scream.)
The third girl's smaller, dark,
She moves with ease among the shelves
And spinners in her long loose coat,
Trailing an air of glamourie.
Her friends behind her whisper.
Slowly she wanders against their
Dragging anchors, among poets, theorists,
Garret-politicians and the witnesses
Of great events, stroking the spines
And faces of another life—
Women and men bird-brained
And flying with fire in their hair.

Two girls in a bookshop want
Their friend to leave. She is
Too precious to them not to claim her,
To haul upon her drifting—she it is
Who threatens them with her
Dipping, dipping, dipping into books.
She is too quiet, too unhysterical
To be Shelley among schoolboys.
Rather she is Maggie Tulliver, with her
Hand upon the handle of the door.

KIRSTY

Her faither says, "Kirsty ma lass,
Dinna haud your heid sae laich."
But Kirsty hings her heid an greits—
For aa the warld ye'd think the warld wis deid—
An gin it were, she wudna gie twa figs,
She's in ower deep tae spare a thocht
For ony frauchtless fykes o ither fowk.
She's up tae here in wae an winna moodge,
Tho she mey catch her daith frae cauld—
It cudna be mair grim nor steyin alive,
O this she's shair. Nae dout the morn's morn
She'll gang about her wark, but daivert-like,
Till Setterday, when some new lad wi bonnie een
Mey set her fleein efter dreams yince mair.

SPATE

The water's reid in spate,
A bonnie breengin flude,
As tho a thousan weemen, seepin bluid,
Had ushed theirsels o aa their luve an hate
Awa upstream. Sae when in time the water's clear
Men that dauner by the burn
'll ken there's mair doun there in dern
Than trout or gedd—an mair tae fear!

JOGGING FOR ETHIOPIA

Drumbrae's the killer.
That long snake climbing out
Of Airthrey's cleft bruises the heel
Like nothing else. Just when you should
Be catching breath at the carse laid out
In smoky-blue below, you're strewing
Pechs and spittle-worms like favours to the wind,
Flinging sweat like tokens from your temples,
Dog-lips drawn back taut against the hammering
Prison-protest in your rib-cage
Crying down the mad belief that this discomfort
Somehow does you good.

           And all to work off
Two-three inches you'd never have put on,
In Ethiopia; where someone twice your age
And half your weight sits very still, and sweats
For fear of drawing off his last reserves;
Whose last reserves are drying up;
Who couldn't run to save his life,
What's left of it to save.

April, 1983

FIVVER POEM

For Alexander Scott (1920-89)

Ye screivit "Calvinist Sang".
An at thae twa words their lane,
That bleezed frae a page ma sicht cudna thole,
Ma fivvered fantice, athout e'en a glent
At the lave o the verse, lowped out
Frae the stane-cauld sheets whaur
Ma body heized in its burnin brash,
An gaed skellopin aff doun the vennel o time
Tae a habble o psalms, sermons an drums
An raggity waffs abune the richteous flytin.

Sterk an sair there on Fenwick muir
The Covenant stude.
Frae Gallowa til the gallus West Bow
Your sang wis heard,
Rairin God-fou as a border-blouster,
Freedom, blin freedom
An nerra-nebbit haliness
Aa in the yae souch.

By Fenwick ma mairtyred flesh has faan
Sindert frae aathin but pyne.
Whaur nou staun the trees skeer-naukit,
Their wirlie snags raxed sklent-weys wi the wind
Like saunts' airms frozen in the moment o prayer,
Ma body founert, an the fivver wis fleyed.

In the lang white hour o ma comin-throu
I jaloused that the warst wis awa;
But saft ower three hunner year a voice whispered:
"Ma name is Legion, for there's a gey feck o us."

13

THE BASTART WEANS

We are the aishan o the warkin class,
Their bastarts, yet we miscaa them, misken
Our mither an our faither.
There is nae justifiein us ava, our thrawn weys,
Our sklent een an our deif, deif lugs.
But we're no blate, our trade's legitimisin
Aa that we can cleik in our cauld clam—
Ay, gar it grup, sir!
Mebbe we're tradin bluid for water, but dinna cast up
Thick an thin tae us, we'll no hae't.
Sleekit, we sleek the weirin-on o Time, his bonnie flanks,
An clap the gowden cauf spune-fed wi siller.
Aa's fine wi us that's wi us, but we cry illegitimate
Aathin else, yea, even unto
Our mither an our faither.
Mindins an girnins an sair-begrutten lees,
That's aa their tale.
Na, we're no perfite, but we hae bettered them
In betterin oursels,
An nou in bourgeois land we sneck our windaes
Ticht an close agin the stour an dirdum.
Mair mansions here nor in our faither's house!
We're douce, content: we buried them afore they
        buried us.

We dinna speak like this: we do not talk thus.
Thon's a message frae a faur-aff land—a place,
A thing we mind the wey o, whiles grace
Wi a dowie smile or wee bit tear—but canny-like:
It disna dae tae awn.
Wha'd awn thon skelet in the press
Wha didna want the past ahint him ayeweys
Proggin at his elbuck for a tanner?

VERY SCOTTISH WEATHER

You watch the weather arrive in droves:
Bitter, fierce, grim and unrelenting.
A batch of Scottish stereotypes perhaps?
When this thought strikes you, idly you begin
To toy with it—November's squalls as images
Of Scottish poetry.
Those angry blasts battering the window
And, in between, the sudden calming lulls
Are such a meeting of extremes they might be
MacDiarmid in full flow.
That rise and fall in the wind—
Is that not the very sound of Sorley intoning,
Breaking off to tell you that the English version
Is no good at all, at all?
This gust snatching and ditching down the street's
A bit of Morgan surely, throwing up all kinds of wonders
In the mind—beer-cans and newspapers
The percussion and confetti of a great parade.
And on the glass, close to your face,
Raindrops track like the little poems
Of MacCaig
Trickling drily
Down the page.

You could go on, but then someone comes in with the tea,
Like your mother, saying,
"You wouldn't want to be out in that."

Heselrig's away, rage and fear and folly having
Boiled to a head, an act of fate, and sealed his own.
On stage is the folded body of a woman, an island
In a sea of pain. She does not stir; the servants
Groan and wail. The wind around the house is rising;
It is May; Scotland's winter is about to roar.
Where is the man that Heselrig came hunting for?
Somewhere in the agony of this dark hour
A legend is being born; but the woman is still,
As though in prayer, or in hiding; her face
To the flags; her body losing grip of itself.
And the blood-cored clout that failed to staunch
Unfurls its bloom from the wound like a rose
At the wame of Wallace's wife.

MORE SNOW ON SCOTLAND

A kirkyard is falling, blanketing all.
It is pure whiteness, whereas
The kirkyard I am in today
Is stoned dull grey and moss-eaten with age.
Now ten billion cold-cross crystal symbols
Of a life and death in Palestine
Smoor every slab, skull, shroud and stark
Unmarked reminder of a folk
Caught out quick on the hills
And frozen solid.

Thrawn beasts you, Scotland! One kirkyard on another
        falls,
And you like sheep in snow-holes still are standing,
Waiting on the thaw, or the last trumpet sounding,
Before you'll acknowledge there's blood in your souls.

FRAGMENT OF AN AUTOBIOGRAPHY

I came to poetry and another view of Scotland
Through MacDiarmid in the year he died.
Pushing twenty-one, I became aware of motion,
Mysteriously familiar, something lumbering through
    the mists
Beyond mastodon and mammoth, and possibilities in
    waves
Rolled in, their distant clashes flooding out
The tannoyed voice announcing his departure.
With a jolt I started, struck by the sudden staring sight
Of my reflected ignorance, idle on the line,
Sitting late and bland and patient in a standing train.
A new-found anger knotted at the neck of my
    exclusive education
And I began to deconstruct and reconstrue.

NATIONALIST SONG

I wouldn't be so sure if I were in your hobnailed boots.
You make me wonder sometimes, swanking
The stretch of your red white and blue braces.
I've seen your stamp before as you serve the bugger right
Muscling in on rank outsiders, I'm fine you're black Jack.
I know your treadmark, and your heroes—

Who wins dares, Dirty Tricks and honest
It's all these bastards understand.
I've heard your trowel bedding broken glass
On little England's walls. You're dangerous.
Social victim maybe, but you're not slow
To put the boot back in—"I tell you what,

That Hitler gave 'em jobs, there's no denying"—
You think you're stepping out when you goosegrease
That one in. You just don't know how right you are.
I don't want your be like us-ness,
Teach the wops a lesson, Ma'am.
Your ecstatic gotcha sickens me . . . .

I hate the triple-cross you bear like a spiteful martyr
On your back, your head, your big white mug,
To flight your darts. I'll have nothing to do
With your rape-inspired erections,
Your fantasies of missile-power.
Keep your queen and country, they are dirt

And how you revel in it.
I draw the line at being imposed upon
By your John Bulldog fascism.
I make my own free stand.
I scattered caltrops once to spike your pride.
I dug pits to trip your arrogance.

MEDITATION

What these monks were doing.
Solitary.
Soul cell-cast for
Time immemorial.

Holy order out of chaos.
Visionary.
Dreamtime maybe
Seeking spirit's dwell.

Peasants' constant clamour no
Illumination.
Finer struggle
Writing on the wall.

Ochrous omen, prison-cave
Confinement.
Bringing forth
The silent squall.

Ignorance in awe of saints bears
Offertory.
Wine and breakfast.
Now I know

PLUS ÇA CHANGE ... 1788–1988

"Poor people are to be advised by the Government: 'Don't shop
when hungry—you may be tempted to buy more than you need'."
The Scotsman, April 1988

A man with a minimum of messages
Spread thinly on the wire mesh of his rattling crate
Is standing pondering the miracle
Of a pyramid of soup tins (built by slaves).
With one stroke deftly aimed—but where?—
He could collapse the whole damned edifice.
It might for a moment ease the swollen anger
In his belly, but it would not wipe the shame
Of being "advised" to keep his lusting eyes
Averted from the food he does not need.

Silent beneath its load another trolley sidles past
Pushed by a woman with accustomed ease.
Things seem to fall, to leap onto her wheeling heap
From the shelves, as she blindly stalks the aisles.
Behind her, led by another bulging trolley,
Slips her husband, sleek and liberated.
The greedy pauper lets them pass, then rattles on,
His din like a tumbril over cobbles.
Ingratitude and ill-disguised contempt
Divide upon his face as he considers them

Against the few pounds from his latest benefit cheque.
He stops again before a mountain-range of cakes
And thinks—a little luxury to restore
His battered pride?
The temptation is too much.

Meanwhile the market-place performs its natural function

As *her* hauteur and *his* indifference check out
With a credit card, and a slave-boy stuffs
Their feast into a dozen bags.

                       From scenes like these
May we detect the regime's state and stage?
A poor man will eat cake tonight; and they,
Like kings.

THEME ON A VARIATION

Do you mind Charlie Breakfast?
His ploy was to earmark (they said)
Young lads with bodies beautiful
And a taste for intellectual drool,
Hold up the bar with them till it shut,
Then casually ask them back for a last
Wee nightcap of whatever they fancied
In his filthy rich orgy flat.
Then—if they were So Inclined—
(And of course they'd have to be blind
To have got that far and not be)
His hand would creep along the settee
For conversation of a different kind.

Be buggered if bacon and eggs,
Sausages, toast, black pudding and tea
Weren't brought you in bed the next day
(So they say)—
That's why he was called Charlie B.

Do you mind old Charlie? Drowned
In a pool of loneliness
Swelled by a bottle or ten
And a tug of the heart complaint. Men
Removing what moved from his commonplace
Home were surprised, most of it junk they found—
Nothing a long-lost relative, lover or friend
Would have claimed, even had one turned up at the end.
Just dust, and some sad magazines, mothballs . . .
And a stink of hearsay that clung to the walls.

INDECENT EXPOSURE

At Pennsylvania Station, New York,
Thanksgiving, 1978.

Some sense slowly hints that there are eyes
On me, tenacious in this shifting graveyard.
Urinals in white rows like elephant jaws
Hold flowing conversations with the open flies
And boneless trunks of pinstripe suits and grey
Old raincoat splashers. Beside me one wee shite's
Having too long shakes gloating and grunting
At his neighbour's shy display.

Poor bastard. Such transport of despair
Was torn from what appalling solitude?
There's something sickening in it, yet
He and I have at least this much to share—
A hope of love and tenderness
In wrinkled limp reality;
Dreaming some more fulfilling role
While this one drains and dribbles to its final emptiness.

Daft, your fascination with this flesh of mine.
It's neither threat nor favour to you, and you're
Irrelevant to it—though I'm not about to slap
Your back with "No hard feelings!", that's for sure.
My pride's at stake in some half-hidden way,
Burning me up in this terminal room;
I'm cursing me rotten with your disgust
As you twist your last gasp into the tomb.

A COUNTRY DIARY

String of pearls about your neck,
Silk and lace upon your breast,
You touch the final eye-line
And slip shoes to your silent repast.

Your gentleman's across the parks,
Catching the air of the early laird.
You watch him go, you watch him
Window-waiting with no word.

He toes a clod as if he knows
It well. You know he fears the land
And the men he pays to work it.
Propriety has him hide-bound.

Never he saw you but as wife,
Fair lady to his high estate.
And never have you held him in sleep,
Close, like a thief, through the night.

He looks as though he could be at ease:
Distant, he seems almost alive.
Ah, but how you have hugged to death
And traced your own body—for love!

How do you own what was never earned,
Or lose what has never been yours?
Your fingers are trembling like shadows
As you button tight your remorse.

INTO EXILE

As I go into exile
I look back and see
Oban losing touch with me.
And behind Oban, Lorn,
Scotland, the world I suppose.
They are wrapped in a pocket
Of me crossing to Mull,
In a small pouch carrying them away from themselves.
I hold them as I lean at the side of this boat,
Looking down at the sea in its fight with men.
And casually, carefully, I empty them in.

'THE MAN OF SORROWS' BY WILLIAM DYCE

In the National Gallery of Scotland, Edinburgh

Christ, when I see you
In your strange robes
In that familiar country
I want to be there too.
Not with you but where you are,
Out among stones,
In broken, lonely places
Where the wind lowps.

Was it not daring of the man
To seat you upon that rock
In that particular wilderness;
To suggest that there
Might be your spiritual home?
Son of God, it was an act of faith
Perhaps, in your humanity
And in the sanctity of earth.

It can't be easy, Christ,
To want so much, to imagine
The world the way you do.
It's hard to leave the warmth
Of arms that hug you, drag you,
Curl their needs around you,
Stifling you back into sense
And the slavery of the possible.

Christ, I know why you're out there
And why you need to be alone,
Suckling your lungs on the barren moor;
I can see you preparing,

Hardening yourself,
And asking forgiveness
For all the sins
You will not have time for.

A PROSPECTOR IN WESTERN
AUSTRALIA TAKES STOCK

I

In the flat of this land
Time stretches and dissolves
In space. Speculation is open-ended.
Tracks stutter, peter out.

Three thousand miles to the north
They are hacking at the lungs of Earth.
Here, the wind is a consumptive cough,
Rising and falling away.
A fire built of the snap-dry scrunts of trees
That litter hereabouts seems
Grotesque, like some medieval cure for fever:
Heat upon heat, blister on a baked skin.
The billy boils and blackens, steam
And smoke drift in the ice-blue air.

II

Flat—at a glance. So was the world
Seen from fifteenth-century Europe.
This land is skilful at deception.
Its alchemy makes all things change—
Their meaning and their worth.
Mounds become mountains;
Boulders signposts;
Flowers promises;
Lakes disappointments.

Creeks cracked with emptiness
Whose sands I sift today for gold
Will flash-flood some time,
Unearthing or burying possibilities,
Spilling themselves like thrown dice
Over old bets.
A millimetre of rain can turn the landscape green;
The outback draws breath, a whispered prayer.
In the north they are cutting down God.

III

Cradling thick tea in stour-grained hands,
I watch the blister blaze and burst.
Not far away there is a place
Where hundreds hunted once for gold;
Shacks, stores, hotels, brothels . . .
There is nothing now but heaps of broken bottles.

The heat upon heat has driven, too late,
A cockroach from its hole.
Purplish, squat, about the size
Of my bruised thumb-nail, it wakes
To find itself in Hell,
Running to left and right along a branch
Laid in a circle of fire.
Mercy occurs to me. I could lift out the branch,
Tip it and its passenger to safety.
But it goes against the grain:
I owe a cockroach nothing.
I sip and watch, as though watching a play,
Its turns and twists, and fall.

THREE EMBRO SONNETS

The Couthie Howff-like Hell

Cwa in frae the cauld: there's a snell skirl swackin
Doun the nicht; speld ye like a herrin, sae she wud,
The windy kimmer bitch! The verra thocht o't siles the
    bluid.
Outby the nicht there's nae cauld comfort lackin.

Inby, nae juke-box beat, nae darts, nae space-machine—
B'Christ, th'invaders cudna breenge in here
Wi ease: ma een can barely penetrate the grunzie beer
I slorp—whit chance thae fremmit fowk ahint their
    screen?

It's grim in here, I'se awn—frae the mirk ye'd
    hauf-believe
We'd sunk ablow the Cougate—we're doun amang
The dribs o Embro in this place. But dinna deave

Yoursel wi thocht o muvin on—afore ower lang
The crack'll cantle up, bodies clout an weave
The warmth an whisky, pit a sheen on th'auld sang.

Hert o Midlothian

Lads that merch frae the east'll no forget
Tae dackle in their step an gaither hate,
Syne wi a glitty gob tae demonstrate
In Embro auld division's bidin yet.

Elder citizens, scunnert by thir ongauns,
Snaff their nebs up at the bitter face

O modren youth—"Sic nesty, in a public place!"
They stotter aff wi flaffin heids an hauns.

"Sic ignorance!"—aweill, in ilka word there's truth.
Thae louns hae splattert history wi their slaiver;
Kissed the hert o stane wi the common mouth.

Time wis when aulder fowk an aa wud favour
Similar dispositions at the Tolbooth.
Gobbin yince wis the daicent-like behaviour.

Gravy

I fell in wi a fella on ma wey tae South Clerk Street
—Telt me he'd juist been dischairged frae the Navy.
I wisna ower keen on the glower he gave me
Sae I didna speir why—'twud hae been indiscreet.

Says he, introducin himsel as Davie,
"Am I in John O Groats?—I've that bluidy sair feet."
"Bristo Square," I says, he says, "Ye've somethin tae
        eat?"
—He wis thinkin o yin o thae cubes tae broo gravy.

"But I'm stervin," he wheenged, "I've no ett the haill
        nicht!
Dae ye no ken a place whaur a man cud get fed?"
I says, "There a chippie doun there on the richt."

He says, "Ye're ma pal, cud ye see us a bed?"
Says I, "Aw c'mon, gie the wife sic a fricht?"
(I wis leein, ye ken—I'm no even wed.)

BLIPS

Wullie's got a brent new weskit,
Bress buttons an a tartan grauvat.
They suit him fine, he had them frae his faither
But he's deid nou—a fair few year back that wud be—
"Ay, wud it?" Wullie's no juist shair;
Then Wullie's no aa there,
But he's lookin swell an gallus in his fancy duds.
"I'm fifty," Wullie says, "I had ma birthday,
Naebody gied me naethin. Here? They gied me—
Aa they gied me—cup o tea."
They're guid tae Wullie here, they're kind,
But Wullie disna ken they're kind—
He's aabody's frien, tho some wud say he's out o order
Menacin daicent fowk the wey he dis
Wi his lost-dug een an the bairnlike grin
Atweesh his mushin pegless fifty-year auld gums.
Sae Wullie shaks your haun:
"Cud ye see us somethin for ma dinner?"
"There ye go, pal, there a pound."
Wull Wullie drink it? Weill, an if he dis,
Hou cud ye grudge it? It wisna drink
Lea's Wullie here amang the café debris,
A bairn in deid man's claes,
Stibble like dried milk dribbles on his chin—
But yin o the countless blips o history. . . .

An there's the bit: wha's out o place,
But time an chance?
Wha's out o order?
Wullie's aa richt,
I think.
Ay, I dae.

EMBRO 1986

Embro, ma toy-toun, wi your fuff o reik at wan o'clock
Blawin your ain fantoosherie: gie ower!
Pack up your wee tin sodgers, an your pan-loaf speak,
An cairry out a cowp on aa your New Town fykes.
Dinna thole that trashtrie, hen, ye daft auld whure,
Ye besom, dinna let them inglish ye out o existence.
Reikie, ye're nae smaik, but juist o late
You scunner me: amang your bourock o stanes an spires,
O fine braid streets an ticht wee closes,
It's nocht but—pittin on the gentry,
Promenadin aa the sins o pride an prejudice
That ither fowk aye luve tae paint ye wi;
Airin graces that are piss-stains on an auld mattress.
Gie ower! Inglishin is yae thing, but anither's
Aa this broun-moued soukin-up tae ony bellygut
That comes tae claim his heritage boakin an belchin
Wi a nievefu o dollars. Charlie Stewart never dreamed
Sae muckle plaid when he stopped by! The garb o
        auld Gaul
Skailin on the streets, an wee macduggies happit roun
Wi scarfs an coats, an tea-towels fit for hingin
By onybody's "ain fireside" frae Baltimore tae Tokyo,
An some bugger frae the Tourist Board is tellin us
That this is us bein leal tae oursels, an makkin jobs
An siller for's forby—an sae are aa Jock Tamson's Bairns,
Dumfounert, meant tae staun on view, an play—the
        whit?—
The fermers, or the tups an jocks, in Hugh MacDiarmid's
        "Cattle Show"?
Gie ower, or else or lang they'll bucht us in the Cougate
Tae be mair at hame, tae ease the thrang, seein as hou
Ye canna muve in Princes Street for pipers.

Embro, in your fancy wine-bars they are fancy-free
        o you.
They dinna ken your auncient youth, your rowth o weys,
Your clarty dignity. They dinna ken, they dinna care.
Gie ower, I say, an pit awa thae toys an baubles.
They mean naethin, naethin neist tae you.
I want tae see your ainsel stravaig your streets yince mair;
I want tae feel your ghaist's braith souchin at ma
        shouther.

GLASGOW 2015

Returning to Glasgow after years out of touch,
Nothing at first seemed changed very much.
But then at the STV centre I found
A clanjamfrie of citizens milling around.
Electronic billboards flashed messages there—
" 'LIVE PHILOSOPHY' pays for minority fare
Game show"—this and others transmitted anew
In Scots and in Gaelic, Chinese and Urdu.
"We announce the repeat of the popular series
On MacFadyen (the Younger)'s 'Low Energy' theories—
To be followed by this year's Saint Andrew's Night Thesis
By Seumas MacIomhair, retiring as preses
Of the 'Front de la Poétique Géophysique' . . ."
I stared at such marvels, unable to speak
Or to credit the latest of these progress shocks—
"SPORTS EXTRA: first Scotswoman signed at Ibrox!"

A HIDDEN HISTORY
OR, THE NEW HEN FACTOR

For Elspeth King

When Aesop's fables intae Scots were pit
By yin that dwalt in auld Dunfermelyne toun—
A dominie o worthiness an wit
By name cried Maister Robert Henrisoun—
Yin o the tales we find him settin doun
Concerned proud Chantecleir, a gentle Cock.
Also, his wife, a bonnie Hen, Pertok.

Tho I mey want the Maister's grace an skeel,
O thae twa birds I hae a further screed.
But first I quote anither makar's spiel,
Tae wit, "Ilk man an mither's son tak heed."
For in this tale baith vanity an greed,
Stupidity forbye, an fausehoods haill,
Are shawn tae be the haudins o the male.

This Chantecleir wan day at dawin's hour
Ris up an gied his "Cock-a-doodle-doo!"
Syne pecked an prinkit aa amang the stour,
Syne crawed again wi kist an chowks puffed fou.
He thocht himsel a verra cordon blue
O cockery—nae ither wis his maik.
E'en Pertok's cry wis but a kecklin craik.

He stude awhile an harkent at the dugs
As like a winter wund they yowled an yammered.
He harkent at the cats an stapt his lugs
As throu his heid their skirlin dirled an hammered.
He heard the murnin kye, the yowes that stammered,

37

The cuddies' bray, the grumphin o the swine.
He thocht: "Whit din is this compared wi mine?"

A gairden grew ayont the fermyaird waa
Whaur clerks an scholars cam tae cogitate,
When frae their darg they wud their een withdraw,
Amang the flouers an trees tae contemplate.
The Cock flew tae the waa—he wisna blate—
An spied a scholar there upon a bink,
Screivin in a buik wi pen an ink.

"Guid sir," quo he, "weill are we met the day.
A noble sang ye are about tae hear.
The noble history o ma race ye'll hae,
As telt by me, the noble Chantecleir.
An gin ye wud apply your honest lear,
Recordin in your jotter as ye sit,
Posterity will hae the benefit."

The clerk turnt ower his page an tuik his pen,
An strauchtwey Chantecleir began tae sing.
There wis nae tale o cocks he didna ken:
O cockish chronicles he wis the king.
He telt o warriors fechtin in the ring,
An hou their spurs they'd win tho they maun bleed.
He praised kenspeckle cocks baith quick an deid.

He telt o courtly luve an chivalry,
O hens baith hamely an o queenly cast;
O hurishness an siclike divilry—
He wis a cock, he hintit, wi a past.
"But nou, gin I but glance—be it neir sae fast—
On young howtowdies, Pertok fits an fizzes.
Masel," says he, "I blame the shameless hizzies."

He telt o cockish poetry an sang
By rhyme royale an terza rima graced;
Aubades an ballads, lyrical an lang,
That shawed the heichest eloquence an taste.
(An Chantecleir had mair o baith nor maist.)
But Pertok an her sisters scorned his haivers;
They'd niver heard sic bluidy clishmaclaivers.

"If this is history," quo they, "it's no the hauf o't.
His method wi the facts is gey selective.
For shair we canna let the blouster aff wi't:
The haill compluther needs a new perspective."
Syne clivver Pertok issued a directive:
"Dear sisters, kilt your coats an luik your best.
I'll gar our guidman flee hame tae the nest."

While Chantecleir yet flirtit wi the scholar,
Unkennin o the stushie at the steadin,
Pertok drew nigh an cleiked him by the collar.
"Your wives," quo she, "are sair in need o beddin.
Haste, haste ye, for eenou they are uncleddin!"
The bluid breenged tae his breeks, he wis that randie,
He wheeched awa at yince for hochmagandie.

Nou Pertok lowps upon the fermyaird waa,
An, smilin at the scholar saft an douce,
"Kind sir," quo she, "ma husband's on a caa—
Some plumbin needin sortit ben the house.
As tae your time he wudna gie abuse
He's speired o me gin I wud tak his place
An feenish aff the history o the race."

Aweill! The clerk yince mair began tae screive
An pointitly transcribit aa she spak.
An sae the Hen, as weill ye micht believe,
Pit things tae richts afore the Cock wan back.

She gied it laldy wi historic crack,
An didna spare the haun o the recorder
In giein her version o the peckin order.

"A cock," says she, "is but an ornament
That luiks an souns weill, but is no essential.
At fertilisin eggs he's diligent,
But disna Science hae the same potential?
His presence in the henhouse is tangential
Tae hou the social system operates.
It's hens that pits the eggs upon the plates.

"It's hens that lays an hens that incubates;
It's hens that raises chickens up frae birth;
It's hens that feeds them, no their feckless mates;
It's hens that scarts for scran amang the yirth;
We're ayeweys thrang, but nane sings o our worth—
Forbye Tod-Lowrie, an ower weill he kens
The sweetest meat is aye upon the hens.

"Nou chivalry an fechtin I disdain.
Upturn them baith an on the nether side,
Like sclaters skelterin aneth a stane,
Murther an rape an mair ye'll find descried.
Screive this intil your buik an dinna hide
The truth frae ony puir unkennin reader."
An solemnly the clerk his promise gied her.

When Chantecleir returned, the clerk wis gane,
Aff tae the leebrary, his buik redd up.
When Pertok telt her man whit she had dune,
By Christ the bugger wisna hauf fed up.
"Whit ye hae telt him maun hae been made up,"
Quo he, "ye're simply no richt qualified."
"A tappit hen," quo she, "needs but her heid.

"Ma dear, ye seem unsiccar an forjaskit.
Ye've mibbe liftit yin ower mony a leg.
But a riddle I hae for ye, an I ask it
Tae check your mental pouers are fine an gleg.
Nou, which cam first, the chicken or the egg?"
"Dinna ken," says he. "Nor I," says bauld Pertok.
"But I ken this, it wis nae a bluidy cock."

MORALITAS

Ah! gentle dames, it gars me greit tae think
Hou lang your richtfu place has been denied.
Ah! gentle sirs, sae pauchtie an perjink,
A guid conceit mey whiles bad conscience hide.
Be shair ye arena deif an blin wi pride.
When ilka cock craws crouse on his ain midden,
Ower lang mey better sangsters bide unbidden.

WOMAN AND DEER

He does not know what she holds for him.
She doesn't know what he brings.
But they have stood now long enough
Watching each other's landscape
From the window, from the hill,
To recognise the change that's taken place—
Something that has crossed between them,
A bar of light, or shadow,
Light and shadow, beam succeeding gloom
As light and shadow pass across a forest floor
Or firelight dances on the ceiling of a room.

The cold has brought him down, and loneliness,
And fear, and another instinct that is somehow
More than natural: as if from a common dream
The two of them had learned to reach
For what they expected least but most desired—
To touch a side of nature beyond fear;
As if in the half-light there's a half-remembered truth—
Of a woman's hand outstretched and cupping
A tentatively probing mouth.

She waits there for him, with her arm, her hand,
Her offer tilted from the curve of her breast.
He sidesteps, sniffs, angles his head, retreats,
Advances, all the nerves and hot-breathed senses
Of his nose and mouth alive; his searching eyes,
The shudder of his delicate approach—
All this is a gift to her for the sweetness
In her palm. And she has reached this moment quite
    alone,
To be with him, and feels her body drenched
In light and shadow to the bone.

Flesh upon flesh. He dips into her hand.
She marvels at the warm wet beauty of that fit,
And now it is with a familiar grace.
Slowly, so as not to startle him,
She lifts her other hand to touch his face.

KINDEACE

The world was huge then. I was proud of my name,
Of what it meant and where it came from.
I was proud of being able to say,
We are from the Highlands, originally.
But then, I knew nothing.

Later, when I had learned much more,
And the world had shrunk,
I became ashamed of the big house, the many acres,
And that my blood had betrayed the blood of others.
Glencalvie people, you were Rosses mostly,
Put out by a Robertson for sheep. Well,
He was on the wrong side of history after all.
Acre by acre his lands were diminished,
His policies parcelled and sold, his house divided
Into flats; his house with a crack at its temple
And a shadow spreading on its brow.
Three summers ago I trod on unruly lawns and felt
My foot sink in the water-fat moss, as into a bog.
If this was not justice, it certainly seemed poetic.
It is sad to see a fine house in decline,
But there is grim pleasure in it too,
Remembering what it was built upon;
God's window-pane engraved with scrapings
From the vale of tears.

Now I stand on the ruins beyond Croick and I
        understand this:
Guilt is not inherited, it comes with knowledge.
Yes, it is just like the old fable—the taste of fruit
In that once perfect garden.

I cannot deny the grief, the emptied glen,
Where regiments of trees are now being raised,
A new and darker occupation.
And although it is not for me to show remorse,
Beating my chest for original sin,
Yet a hard stone is scratching at my heart,
Glencalvie people: THE WICKED GENERATION.

ON HUGH MACDIARMID

I have sat among old men who were young
When he was old, and been amazed at how,
When his name was named
Or mentioned or invoked,
It was as if an unseen puppeteer reached down
Through the mess of glasses and the smoke
To the tangle of their strings and jerked
Them all at once with a cunning force
That made some raise their drinks and some their fists
And some throw back their heads and laugh.
Genius, one declared; charlatan, roared another;
Friend, a third said, quietly but quite clear
Amid the pandemonium. I watched,
And something I believed about myself
Was confirmed in them: once touched by him,
Nothing could ever be the same.

I did not know him till he died.
Before that—strange to think it now—
A name was all he was to me,
A vaguely heard of fact of Scottish life.
But when I read the news, I understood at once
That someone great had gone, and it was up to me
To find out who, and why.
He challenged everything, and a challenge
Was in everything he did,
The hardest and the simplest being
To be yourself.
Some say saviour, some false prophet, and some
Remember friend. I have my doubts and my suspicions
Just like anyone, but of this I'm sure,
That what he did was change my life,
He changed my life.

FLYTE

For Robert Crawford

You, ay, you with your
Semi-conductors and your
St Andrews kaleidoscopes,
Your Lord Kelvins and your John Logie Bairds,
Yes, it's you I'm talking to.
Who the hell do you think you are
And what travesty of Scotland do you imagine you're in
With these erotic Carnousties,
Erotic picnics?
You've obviously been taking drugs,
So it was no surprise to discover that you
Teach in a university.
Scottish literature?—you wouldn't know it
If you stepped in it.
I've been through all your so-called books
And I've not found a single antler yet.
In fact scarcely any of the things
That made this country what it is are mentioned
Except in a sneering, condescending kind of way.
Cultural smut—that's what that is;
You should be made to wash out your mucky wee pen
        with soap.
Even when you write about rain you somehow contrive
To make it anti-Scottish.
Your Strathgawkies and Strathgowkies,
Sterts and Stobies—
People don't talk like that, you know.
Well, obviously you don't.
Sharawaggi, I mean to say!
Who are you trying to impress?

And another thing—
Don't think I'm writing this because I have to.
You and your nonsense may have come into my head
For God only knows what reason
Just as I was dropping off, but it was my choice
To rise from my warm bed at five to midnight
And find this scrap of paper to scribble on,
Because I knew I wouldn't sleep until I'd got this down,
And you clean out of my system.

So.
You think you're smart but you don't fool me,
Mr Craw-bloody-ford.
Next you'll be telling us you know
What kind of noise a noise like a turnip makes.

LITCRIT

Why was he considered good?
Was it that his poems stood
For things secreted deep within
All of us—unoriginal sin?

Or is it on the other hand
That Larkin and his poems stand
For what we try to shutter out?—
Loneliness. Guilt. Fear. Self-doubt.

MAKAR O THE WARLDS

Lang efter the lowe had gane
O the politics an the polemics
Still his poems cud be seen
Up there,
The *ceol mor* and the perfite
Wee sangs, arcin across the universe
Like space-ships,
Like starns.

IN LANARKSHIRE

I met a man who walked the roads
And crossed the hills
And walked the roads
In Lanarkshire

And everywhere he walked
Observing this
Admiring that
He followed all the hidden veins
Of Lanarkshire

Lanarkshire is not
Considered beautiful he said
But I've considered it
Along the old red roads
And that it is

He learned the lore of all the birds
How they were called
And how they called
And how the starling mimicked all
The other birds of Lanarkshire

He'd gather stories when he stopped
For cups of tea
Of miners and the Covenant
And other ghosts that haunt
The weary ways of Lanarkshire

And everywhere he went
He took two notebooks
Stuffed with words
Verses that spoke the miles on miles
He'd walked through Lanarkshire

Those notebooks filled with verses
Full of places
Full of people
All Lanarkshire
Was in his verses

And his verses all contained
In Lanarkshire
They followed faithful as a dog
I'd like to get a dog I'd like
The company he said

Then all of Lanarkshire
One day might get
In to that dog
I had to check a map
For all the tiny places he had been

I saw no evidence of maps
Upon his person but I saw
The headings on the pages
Of his notebooks
Underlined in red

Were names of other books
Ezekiel Isaiah
Amos Jonah Lamentations
Lanarkshire it seemed
Was full of prophets

I said your verses
Should be framed and up on walls
In tea-rooms and in pubs
In old hotels
To show where you have been

And how the roads and hills
Can get on walls
And into frames
And out of frames
In Lanarkshire

A SPACE BETWEEN THE YEARS

In Biggar each New Year a huge fire is lit in
the middle of the High Street

Hogmanay. All night we reel from house to house
Dimly observing on each less graceful pass
How the great bonfire folk come miles to see
Has blazed and lowered, diminishing by degree

The shadows that it casts on walls and cobbles.
Toast after toast is raised, and our own bottles
Fall dram by dram as we dogmatically return
The hospitality. And still the timbers burn.

We are together, for the first time, for the Bells.
An occasion, or a turning-point, is how it feels;
You and me dancing in the street like wedding guests;
Emigrés from other happy and less happy feasts.

At last we reach a stage where we can go
No further, trip in a last untangling tango
Into a room full of out-of-focus figures seated
Round another, smaller fire; again we're greeted,

And crumbling slabs of cloutie-dumpling fall
Like cliffs in on a belly-sea of alcohol.
It's another year! And another one's gone by. We're
Older, all of us, but it's as if we've always sat here

And always will. So lift your glass again, kiss
And make up whatever future you desire, before the mist
That fills the space between the years departs.
Familiar hopes: good health, and mended, or unbroken,
        hearts.

I feel, shortly after the dark despairing bit
Of "Ae Fond Kiss", the old year well up in the pit
Of me: far too much whisky and not enough water
To quench it. I fall upstairs to the bathroom, loiter

On the edge, the rim, waiting for something to begin.
It does. I let it all come out as below me voices sing
In harmony of warring sighs and groans. I roar,
But they drown me out in a touching last encore.

The noise and pain subside. Coiled, wet, blind, I'm lying
There, and suddenly, I don't know why, I find I'm crying,
Hard up against the cool, impersonal porcelain of the
        toilet,
My face imprinted on and by the cording of the carpet.

I'm in some state, but in time it's peaceful, safe, so why
Am I afraid? Why does the past refuse to say goodbye
Even when you come, concerned, to ask if I'm okay;
And yes, as though denying everything, yes, yes, I say.

STILL LIFE WITH OLD DOG

You've merged, the pair of you,
As they say you always do:
Master and hound, beast and man.

One of you has had a tied-up life:
Told to stay; barred from shops
Because the other isn't blind;
Tethered to lamp-posts in the rain;
Nervous of claps from kindly strangers;
Shying from barking boys; shivering while
He wanders the aisles in the library.
Black-eyed outside the butcher's
You've tried not to dream the great escape,
A stream of sausages flying about your earflaps:
The very thing he's seen time and again
In the Fun Section of *The Sunday Post*.

Sundays. An hour a week, in all weather,
The heathen one of you waits for the end
Of the service, crouched at the kirkyard gate.
Before he returns you always see him, alone,
Cap in hand, shuffling through the headstones
To that one you're not trusted to respect.
Each day he lets you off in the woods
But you don't go far these late afternoons.
Coming in out of the rain and cold
Your shabby coats steam like leaky geysers
And it's hard to tell which of you smells
More like an old wet dog.

In the pub you're part of the local colour,
Visiting tables and the open fire,
Muzzled by crisp pokes, licking whisky

From the hanging teat of his finger.
Neither of you drinks a lot, it goes
To your head, you can both still snap
If irritated. But mostly you're as you are,
One sat, one stood at the bar, not talking
Among yourselves. Who knows what memories distil
Behind the dark eyes and their soft, occasional stir?
When you slump for a while, who'd fathom the twitch
Of your dreams, or what's meant by the odd wee growl?

One of you has grandchildren who visit
Sometimes. The other may have who don't,
But even if they did, they'd look only
A bit like you. And then there was her that would never
Come into such a place. Was she genteel, or afraid?
Did she waste words on you as he never does,
Just for the sound of someone to talk to?
You were brought up by the flat of his hand,
And he by the Book with its great divide:
One born sinning, the other learning the hard way.
You're such a pair it's not easy to think
Of religion coming between you;

Not easy to believe in a day, sooner now
Rather than later, when one of you will go
To meet his Maker, and the other will stay.

THE BLUES AT BROWNSBANK

They come before dawn. Packed in stiff kind cardboard,
They sit outside the blue door where the slug-trails
Gleam beneath the thistle-knocker. Stone chips
Squabble briefly with the post van's wheels;
Aggregating with the growl of lagged
Hot water bubbling in the tank above my head.
A label in the darkness: Red Lick Records,
Porthmadog, Gwynedd, Wales. Another hour in bed.
Sheep pass. I doze, then rise and fill the long white bath
Where Valda's oils and henna sachets still tilt at youth.
Johnny Shines, Big Walter, Lightnin', they'll have to wait.
The greeshoch whispers rumours in the grate.

Twenty Hugh MacDiarmids watch me dress,
Stir up the ashes and a stubborn glow, a flame.
I start to fit my day between the portraits, books,
His pipes, her wally dugs, the desk she built for him,
The doocots where he filed his thoughts away.
Against the catalogued accretions of their thirty, nearly
Forty years, my own familiars rest, strangely assured:
A frog, with fishing-rod, perpetually, unwearily
Content that nothing bites; my grandparents in the
        Twenties,
In *their* twenties, forever laughing in the frame; Quixote's
Eight-inch wooden stance, his unenquiring eye;
A quaich, a gift that I remember someone by;

A small, soft, ugly, hairy creature like a brownie,
Keeper of the peats and fireplace (a raffle prize);
Postcards—Lanzarote, Bellany, Morrocco, Greece—
And books, books, more and more, thickening in rows
I always mean to thin, but never do. And now these
        blues,

Black circles within squares, black men with their
    bottlenecks
And slides, in from the cold. Along with them I bring
The morning light draped powdersoft on Broughton
    Heights,
The grass starched white with cranreuch, greylags ticked
And arrowed on the pale November sky. Stacked
Lorries hum and rumble on the road to Biggar,
    southbound;
Unseen from here they are unreal, divorced, mere sound.

Like Chris and Valda, these blues come at me
From a different age. I'm grabbing what's left of it.
The L.P.'s dead, but still these last few stiffs
Arrive to grace the Garrard deck, the amp, the deep-set
Goodman speakers. *'Is it all right to put the stereo in?'*
(I live in a museum.) *'He kept his player underneath the
    bed,*
On casters.' I crank the volume up: a hotel room
In Nineteen-Thirties Texas, Robert Johnson bowed
Across the strings, next-door the phonograph
To hold his voice, the men from A.R.C. who hold their
    breath.
Crackle. Then, from floor to wooden ceiling here, the air
Is filled to bursting with his anguish and despair.

What links a house in Clydesdale to this weird combine
Of innocence, iniquity, melancholy, sheer exuberance?
In Johnson's blues, if anywhere, extremes meet, disturb
The mind like gargoyles grinning next to kneeling saints.
An overwhelming sense of woe is overwhelmed by
Sensuality. I hear him, dead at twenty-seven, holler
Like a hellhound in this room where a poet slept
Above the means for playing Gustav Mahler.
Greenwood, Mississippi, 'Thirty-Eight—it came to this:
A jealous husband poisoning whisky maybe even as

He sang 'You *can squeeze my lemon till the juice run
        down my leg';*
And Robert dying on his hands and knees, barking like
        a dog.

In Valda's room a mouse is dead beneath a spring;
Blood wells in its lug, stops after one bright drop
Has fallen like a ruby on the dull linoleum.
My guilt will rub and rub to out that spot,
But still I won't feel good about the tiny corpse
When I free it from the trap into the ash.
I fear being overrun by the little things,
Losing the place, perspective, sense of scale, of touch.
'*D'ye mind the wife? She'd awfy rid hair.*' '*She dyed it.*'
'*I was never in love with him. I loved him.*' Valda said it.
How different love and being in love were only she
        could say.
'*I got a rich man's woman, but she livin' on a poor
        man's pay.*'

On a morning such as this she'd wake before him,
Start to reassemble all the debris
Of the night before. At the door she'd find
A dozen Bluebell matches, and the box maybe,
Where he'd tried to strike a light; nearby the pipe, tobacco,
And further on an empty bottle, the coat discarded
At the gate; finally his teeth; all the signs of a good night,
Or a hard one. Back in past the thistle (unregarded),
At the tail-end of this bombed and littered road,
Would lie the intellect, the mass of hair upon the head
Upon the pillow of Scotland's greatest poet. She'd
        assume
He'd sleep it off, the burden of his people's doom.

Those years you were in Whalsay, Johnson
Trudged the Mississippi roads, arriving, disappearing,

Pouring out the devil's magic of his songs.
Lying on a raised beach, trying to get at the uncaring
Stones, did you pick up the soundwaves of that eerie voice
Crying *'Come on in my kitchen'*, *'Love in vain'*?
Words flood in from everywhere: poets sending messages
Not from the sense of language but its strain.
The sleevenotes tell how hearing Robert Johnson's
Playing could make women weep, men too. For those
    runs,
That pitch, you'd sell your soul or break your heart.
Only pure evil, some believed, could sound so sweet and
    sharp.

A yellow moon hangs like a lantern in the dark.
You wait beside a crossroads at the midnight hour.
Nervous fingers strum and pick a little piece.
And now there comes the shadow of the one you play for,
Looming like a boulder; he takes the instrument,
Tunes it with an ear for exactly what perfection's like,
Plays a piece, and hands it back with not a word,
The ghost of a smile. Your hands touch at the neck.
In that brief exchange two certainties are found:
The blues are yours, all chords, all meaning, every sound
A gift and curse to you, nightmare and dream;
And, who the stranger is and what his fee has been.

In Scotland a man might rest a while one day
Upon a mound in summer, to bathe in the heat,
And feel a weariness come over him, drowse,
Sleep; and be carried by the fairies deep
Into the hill, drained and slaved by them,
Filled like a vessel magic-full, with secret powers,
Hidden knowledges, sight beyond the sight of other men.
Stirring awake, he'd find he'd stayed a couple of hours
Too long, and stumble home to the wonder of his
    guessing,

Greying friends and family. He'd been considered dead, missing
Seven long years, vanished utterly. In time to come the face
Of the earth would shun him, wary of his skills, his new grace.

MacDiarmid, you returned from Shetland as one
Who had gone into the stones, conversed with them
And overcome their silence and indifference. Scotland
Preferred you at a distance, but you came home
Out of devilment, and need, knowing your country
Could not do without you. (Fine and heroic it may be
To suffer for your art, but to suffer for another's,
As Valda did, in some ways more impresses me.)
Here, at Brownsbank, you settled finally with the stour—
But still sending out odd letter-bombs, sniping from the door.
And in the music of the Delta sometimes I get clear
Echoes of your lives, ricochets from eternity to here.

What do I touch when I touch an object here?—
This lamp, this chair, this book with the note in his clear
Downsloping hand that says 'To Valda with all my love.
Where would I—or Scots poetry—have been without her?'
What do I feel when I feel nothing of their presence?
This place is better than haunted, it is real, inhabited;
Inanimate, it has not felt the passing lives of cottars,
Cottars' wives, folk of the land who sucked, shat, mated,
Fought, loved, died, age after age, after them a poet
And a poet's wife, a widow, now me, and through it
All we are nothing to the stones. Though we build a space
From them for our lives, our lives are nothing. This we must face.

Where will we go from here? Where will I go?
Who will be here in a hundred years, will this house
Be here? Impossible to tell, or what, but worms, the walls
May disgorge in a slow seepage of stone-stored noise—
A cacophony perhaps, composed of Valda, Chris,
MacDiarmid, the Delta blues and Mahler—writers
Not in residence—rodents, crows, the wind in flow,
Spring lambs under whaups and peeweets, oyster-catchers,
Another crop of winter geese on the barley stubble,
Scots words still thick on the land, rough, kind, capable
Language enduring against the odds, douce, dour cratur—
This is one way of listening out for the future.

But what if one sound replaces all the others, drowns
Them in its appalling, unrelenting dominance?
What's likely to survive, not in a hundred years,
Not in a thousand, but in a million? What, but silence?
As when the tree falls deep in the forest—if it falls—
What will be heard is what we can't imagine:
Nothing. The sound of other planets. Nothing. Like a
        stylus
Poised above a record, or when the record-player's broken.
Like the sound the road makes empty of cars and lorries.
Not like the snow falling, but the sound of what it buries.
Silence. This is all there will be, and you were right,
MacDiarmid, thus to end that long, intoxicated night.

*   *   *

A landscape without sound is like a country without
        names—
Mappable but desolate, inhuman, cold. 'I didn't see a
        soul
All day on the hills' would be a chilling tale if there was
Nobody to tell it to. To name what surrounds us is all
We can do: Valda, Chris, Robert, you've left your signs,

And we must make what we will of them, for in due time
All we, too, can be is be remembered. This is our fate,
Or not, as it may turn out. Remember, lest we be forgot.
Though the dead are saved on vinyl or in books survive
It's what we, the living, make of them that keeps them live.

SOUND-SHADOW

Come in, come in.
But you don't, so should I assume
You're not receiving me?
Come in. Nothing.
But if my words won't stretch to you,
Where do they go?
Come in. No,
You're not responding,
Or I'm not. Maybe our worried syllables
Are meeting somewhere off the map,
Discussing us, unheard, unmonitored.
Anyway, for now, it seems I've lost you.

I'm weary, lay down the headset,
Don't even reach for the on/off
Switch since the airwaves are dead
With or without it.
If there was fuzz there'd be hope,
If there was interference at least
I could think that someone was out there.
But this, this is the worst, this space
Swiped clean of clicks, whirrs, roars,
Crackle. Not even a few half-scrambled
Phrases fading in, in an unfamiliar accent,
Or a language I don't understand.

How big are we talking? How far
Does it reach? How wide this silence,
How high the barrier?
How long do I have to keep on listening
To get beyond the gloom, out
Into the sunlight of your voice again?